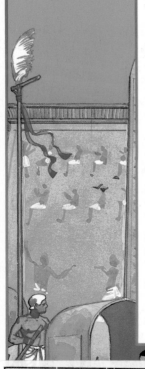

SERIES EDITOR   DAVID SALARIYA
EDITOR   APRIL McCROSKIE

W FRANKLIN WATTS

First published in 1996
by Franklin Watts
a division of the Watts Publishing Group Ltd
96 Leonard Street
London EC2A 4XD

This edition published 2000

ISBN 0 7496 3803 6
Dewey Classification 932

Printed in Belgium

A CIP catalogue record for this book is available from the British Library.

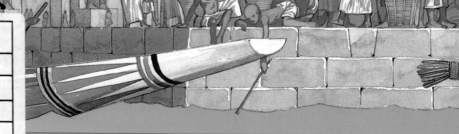

Leisure & Community Services

Please return this item by the last date stamped below, to the library from which it was borrowed.

Renewals
You may renew any item twice (for 3 weeks) by telephone or post, providing it is not required by another reader. *Please quote the number stated below.*

Overdue charges
Please see library notices for the current rate of charges for overdue items. Overdue charges are not made on junior books unless borrowed on adult tickets.

Postage
Both adult and junior borrowers must pay any postage on overdue notices.

15 MAR 2004	– 6 JUN 2013	
– 4 APR 2005		
– 4 AUG 2005		
– 7 OCT 2006		
– 1 MAR 20	**Renewals**	
1 2 JUL 2008	**0333 370 4700**	
1 6 JUL 2009	arena.yourlondonlibrary.net/	
0 2 JUL 201	web/bromley	
2 3 APR 2012		

739.96

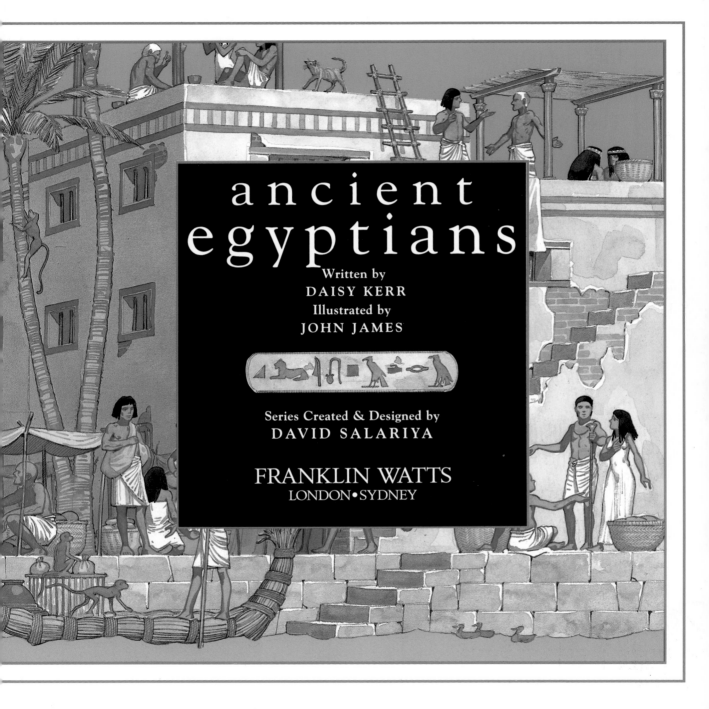

ancient egyptians

Written by
DAISY KERR

Illustrated by
JOHN JAMES

Series Created & Designed by
DAVID SALARIYA

FRANKLIN WATTS
LONDON·SYDNEY

The ancient Egyptians lived in north

Africa. From around 3100 BC, they developed a rich, powerful civilisation that lasted for thousands of years. Egyptian farmers grew plentiful crops and craftworkers built magnificent monuments. Egyptian pharaohs led mighty armies and scientists made many important discoveries in mathematics and technology.

Egyptian power collapsed when Roman armies invaded in 30 BC. But Egyptian skills and traditions survived for many more years.

Egypt lay at the crossroads of several important trade routes linking north Africa with Arabia, the Middle East and lands around the Mediterranean Sea.

Over 90 per cent of Egypt is desert. The only fertile, well-watered land is in the northern delta region, and along the banks of the River Nile.

Ancient Egyptians

divided their country into two different regions – 'Deshret' (the Red Land) and 'Kemet' (the Black Land).

Deshret was a dry, stony desert. No-one could live there, but it was rich in minerals. Tough Egyptian labourers were sent to quarry granite and limestone for statues and temples, copper for weapons and tools, and gold, turquoise and carnelian for jewellery.

Kemet was very different. There, you could see villages and fields of rich, black mud along the banks of the River Nile. All living things in Egypt depended on the waters of the Nile.

Every year, in July, Nile floods covered the fields with water and rich, fertile mud.

In October, the flood waters retreated. Farmers ploughed the fields and sowed seeds.

Workers dug new irrigation channels to bring more river water to the fields.

In April, the corn was ready to harvest. Farmers cut it with flint-toothed sickles.

An Egyptian farmer's year

was divided into three seasons – floods, seed-sprouting and harvest. At flood-time their fields were under water, so they could not work on the land. They had to work on government building projects like a new road, or a pyramid tomb. Egyptian farmers grew wheat to make bread, and also fruit and vegetables like figs, grapes, onions and garlic. Some farmers grew palm trees for thatch, others grew flax to make linen cloth.

Digging stick

Some fields were ploughed by oxen. Others were cultivated using digging sticks. Seed was scattered by hand, then trampled into the mud by animals.

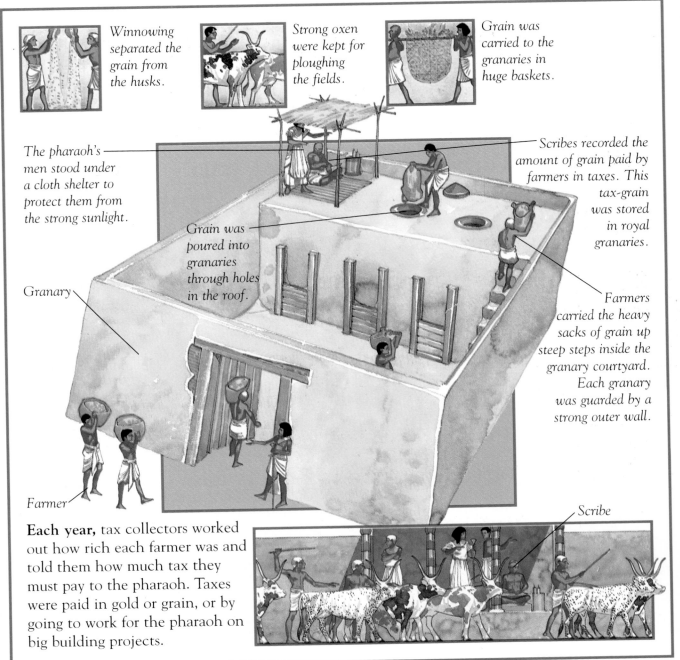

Winnowing separated the grain from the husks.

Strong oxen were kept for ploughing the fields.

Grain was carried to the granaries in huge baskets.

The pharaoh's men stood under a cloth shelter to protect them from the strong sunlight.

Scribes recorded the amount of grain paid by farmers in taxes. This tax-grain was stored in royal granaries.

Grain was poured into granaries through holes in the roof.

Granary

Farmers carried the heavy sacks of grain up steep steps inside the granary courtyard. Each granary was guarded by a strong outer wall.

Farmer

Each year, tax collectors worked out how rich each farmer was and told them how much tax they must pay to the pharaoh. Taxes were paid in gold or grain, or by going to work for the pharaoh on big building projects.

Scribe

Egyptian families provided

jobs, love and security for their members.
Village men worked in the fields or in craft
workshops. Women cooked, cleaned, spun
thread, wove cloth and brewed beer at
home. Rich women organised servants, too.

Egyptians married young, but many people
died before they were 30. Men were killed
in battle and women died in childbirth.
Egyptian doctors used herbal remedies, but
anyone might catch a deadly disease, be
stung by a scorpion or eaten by a crocodile.

Egyptians married
for love and for
money, too.
A rich bride
was highly prized.

Laws protected
women. They
could get a divorce
if their husbands
treated them badly.

Most children
were taught skills
at home. Boys
learned farming
or craft work,
girls learned
household and
child care skills.

*The Egyptians did not
use money. Families
bartered (swapped)
goods at the market.*

Egyptian families
hoped to have lots
of children, to help
run their houses,
workshops and farms.

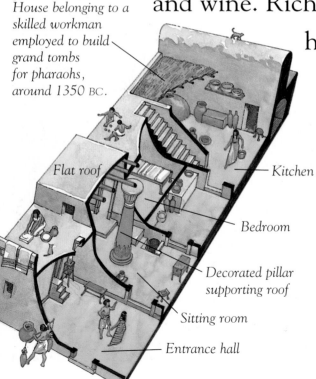

Clay model of a house, showing doorway, window, courtyard, outside stairs and flat roof. Models like this were placed in tombs.

House belonging to a skilled workman employed to build grand tombs for pharaohs, around 1350 BC.

Ordinary houses had earth floors and plaster-covered walls. Most had two or three rooms and a courtyard, used for cooking. Furniture was simple, too – a bed, a few chairs or stools, some wooden chests and pottery jars for storing olive oil, grain and wine. Rich families had more luxurious homes, built on two or three floors. They had separate bathrooms and lavatories.

Flat roof

Kitchen

Bedroom

Decorated pillar supporting roof

Sitting room

Entrance hall

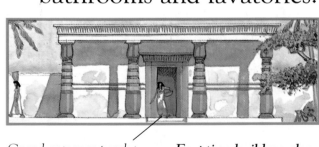

Grand entrance porch of a house built for a noble family around 1320 BC. The house had many big rooms and a large garden.

Egyptian builders also constructed massive palaces, temples and pyramid tombs. Turn the page to see a pyramid being built.

Kitchen area

Basket-maker

Oven

Palm-leaf thatch

Flat roof

Builder

Mud bricks drying
in the sun

15

Left to right: Overseer; Irrigation manager; Controller of state granaries; Chief steward; Director of building works; Army commander; Controller of nome (province); Chief scribe; Courtier.

Courtiers and other rich people wore long tunics of fine pleated linen, which felt cool and comfortable in Egypt's hot weather. They also liked to wear elegant wigs, and jewellery made of gold, turquoise and lapis lazuli – a blue stone.

Egypt was ruled by powerful kings, called pharaohs. The Egyptians believed he was the son of god. He was the chief priest. He was the army commander and head of the government, giving orders to officials and scribes. He supervised law and order, tax collection, food supplies and trade, irrigation and mining. The pharaoh also held audiences at his splendid royal court, where he listened to requests from top officials, nobles and visitors from distant lands.

Making offerings of food and drink to gods and goddesses in the temples.

Listening to reports about the country from the vizier (head of administration).

Inspecting major public works – pyramids, roads, ditches and canals.

The pharaoh was also a war-leader. It was his duty to plan campaigns and command the army. The most famous warrior-pharaoh was Rameses II (1279-1213 BC).

The word 'pharaoh' comes from *perr-aa*, which means 'great house'.

Pharaohs received tribute – presents of rich treasures like gold and cedarwood – from conquered lands.

Documents authorised by the pharaoh were stamped with his seal.

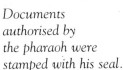

Musicians entertained the pharaoh and his guests with songs.

Favourite instruments included the flute, zither and harp.

Dancers made music with clappers, bells and kitharas.

On hunting trips, Egyptians chased water birds, snakes and, sometimes, crocodiles.

Double flute player   *Kithara player*   *Harp player*   *Lyre player*

The Egyptians enjoyed their leisure time.

Pharaohs and nobles held great banquets, where they entertained guests with delicious food, music and dancing. Ordinary people also enjoyed dances and songs. They had picnics and hunting trips beside the river, too.

Honoured guests

Perfumed wax

Pharaoh

Women guests were offered cones of perfumed wax which melted in their hair.

The pharaoh and his guests were entertained by dancers and acrobats. Many dances were full of leaps, handstands and somersaults.

Guests ate roast duck, stewed deer, lettuce and onion salads, and date and honey cake.

Pharaoh's servant

Egyptian toys. These painted clay rattles were filled with seeds and beads.

Egyptians enjoyed listening to storytellers, watching jugglers and conjurers, and playing board games like 'senet' (similar to modern draughts). Children played with rattles, tops, dolls and wooden animals on wheels.

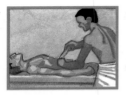

The lungs, liver, intestines and stomach were taken out of the body to stop it rotting.

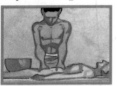

The body was packed with natron (soda) and left for 40 days in a natron-filled trough to dry out.

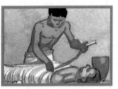

Finally, the body was wrapped in resin-soaked bandages to keep the dried flesh and bones in place. If a bit of body dropped off or rotted away, the embalmers replaced it with linen pads and bits of wood.

The ancient Egyptians

feared death, and wanted to live for ever. They believed that if a dead person's body was preserved, their spirit would be preserved too, giving them everlasting life.

At first, the Egyptians preserved bodies by burying them in the desert. The dry sand stopped them rotting away. Later, pharaohs and rich people paid to have their bodies preserved as mummies, by embalming. The word 'mummy' comes from the Arabic word for black tar – people thought mummies looked as if they were covered in tar. The Egyptians also mummified their favourite animals, especially pet cats. They buried them in special temple cemeteries.

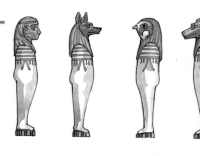

Amulets (small carvings), were placed between the layers of bandages. Egyptians believed these helped preserve the body.

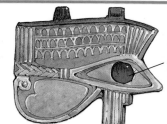

Amulets shaped like the 'wadjet' eye were thought to protect the mummy.

The mummy case was painted with many magic spells, written in hieroglyphs, to help the mummy's spirit in the life after death.

The body was wrapped in layers of shrouds, then placed in a mummy-shaped inner coffin. Often this was painted with a portrait of the dead person's face.

Turn the page to see inside a mummy case.

Once inside the inner coffin, the mummy was placed in a strong, rot-proof outer case. This might be made of wood or stone.

After the lungs, liver, stomach and intestines had been taken from the body, they were placed in tightly sealed canopic jars and buried in the mummy's tomb.

Pharaohs' bodies were ferried across the River Nile from the east bank, where the royal palaces were, to the west bank – the Kingdom of the Dead. Priests and mourners went along, too.

The funeral boat was made of cedar wood. It was about 45 metres long, and powered by rowers. It was guided by double steering oars.

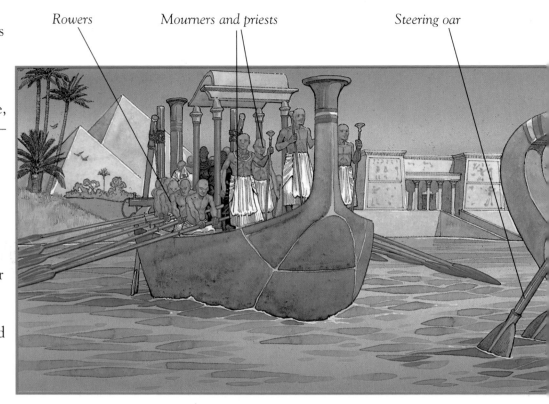

Rowers

Mourners and priests

Steering oar

Funerals took place on the west bank of the Nile. Once a mummy was buried, its spirit began a new life in the Kingdom of the Dead. Tombs were decorated with paintings of the dead person hunting, worshipping the gods and enjoying family life. Tombs had everything the

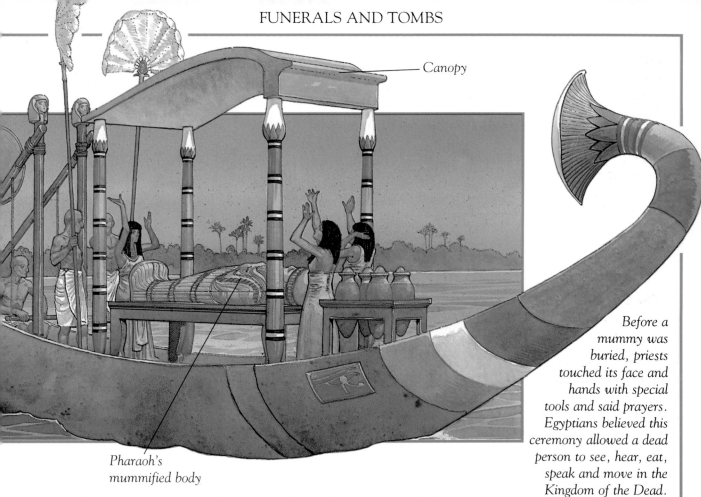

Canopy

Pharaoh's
mummified body

Before a mummy was buried, priests touched its face and hands with special tools and said prayers. Egyptians believed this ceremony allowed a dead person to see, hear, eat, speak and move in the Kingdom of the Dead.

OPENING OF
THE MOUTH CEREMONY

dead person might need – food and drink, clothes, weapons and games. Models of houses, boats, farm animals, servants and companions were also placed in the tomb, so the dead person could enjoy these too.

Hieroglyphs

Priests and scribes could read and write hieroglyphs – a system of picture writing with over 700 symbols.

Boys who wanted to be priests had to study hard at school. They were beaten if they did not listen.

The Egyptians worshipped

many gods and goddesses. They built temples to honour them, where priests and pharaohs offered clothes, food and water three times a day. They carved statues to show their many forms like Horus, the hawk-like sky god, Sakhmet, the lion-headed goddess of battle, or Bastet, a proud cat. Some were worshipped in only one place, like crocodile-god Sobek, who lived in the river. Others, like sun-god Amun-Re, were worshipped everywhere.

Shrine

Temple

Temples were homes for gods and goddesses. Each temple had a shrine – a special holy place, where the spirit of the god or goddess lived. This spirit was represented by a huge statue.

On festival days, (right) statues were carried through the streets by priests. Often, the statues were hidden inside a shrine – they were thought to be too holy for people to see.

Potter

Carpenter

We know about Egyptian towns because their remains, like Kahun (built around 1895 BC) and Deir el Medina (built around 1350 BC) have been excavated (dug up).

Craftworkers

used simple tools – flint drills, wooden mallets and bronze saws. Yet their monuments have survived for almost 5,000 years. Most artists and craftspeople worked for the government, building and decorating massive palaces and tombs. Other skilled people worked at home, making sandals, moulding pottery or carving wood. Gold-workers, wig-makers, jewellers and glass-blowers made and sold their goods in towns.

Sandal-maker

River Nile

Rooftop shelter

Weaver

Spice seller

Palm tree leaves
used as thatch

Cloth hung over
balcony to bleach
in the sun

Basket-maker

Scribes were officials who recorded events, helped collect taxes, and wrote down the pharaoh's orders.

Governors of nomes (provinces) had the power to make a man work for the pharaoh, or join the army.

Around 3100 BC, Pharaoh Menes

united the two earlier kingdoms of upper and lower Egypt into one large nation. Then the Egyptians fought and conquered peoples, in what is now present-day Libya, Syria and Iraq. Egyptian troops were tough, well-fed and fit. Soldiers fought on foot, using bows and arrows, spears, axes and clubs.

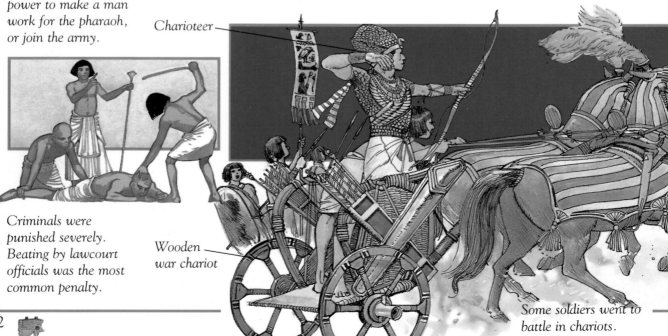

Charioteer

Wooden war chariot

Some soldiers went to battle in chariots.

Criminals were punished severely. Beating by lawcourt officials was the most common penalty.

Battles were bloody and if enemies were captured, they became slaves.

Egypt was difficult to govern. There were few roads, and travel by river was slow. Even urgent messages could take weeks to arrive. So, pharaohs divided the kingdom into provinces, called 'nomes', and relied on governors to help them rule.

Spear

Battle axe

Short wool or linen kilt

Shield

Bare feet

WEAPONS

1 Short sword (copper)
2 Spear head (bronze)
3 Spear head (bronze)
4 Scimitar (sword with curved blade)
5 Club with sharp point
6 Battle axe
7 Wooden club

Egyptian soldiers fought mostly on foot. They had no armour. Instead, they defended themselves with large wooden shields.

Ancient Greeks and Romans who visited Egypt between 500 BC-AD 200 wrote descriptions of Egyptian civilisation.

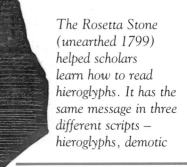

French army commander Napoleon Bonaparte invaded Egypt in 1789. He took many Egyptian remains back to France.

A lot of evidence has survived to tell us about life in ancient Egyptian times. The pharaohs' magnificent pyramid tombs still stand. There are wall paintings, carvings and statues, hieroglyphic inscriptions and temples and palaces. Books written on papyrus (paper made from reeds) by Egyptian scribes tell us about ancient beliefs and ceremonies. We can also learn about the ancient Egyptians from travellers like the Greek writer Herodotus, who visited the country around 500 BC.

The Rosetta Stone (unearthed 1799) helped scholars learn how to read hieroglyphs. It has the same message in three different scripts – hieroglyphs, demotic (everyday Egyptian language, which used letters) and ancient Greek.

Two famous Egyptian names in hieroglyphs and letters.

P T O L M I I S

K L I O P A D R A

Today, archaeologists use scientific techniques and modern materials (like plastics and new types of glue) to try and preserve ancient Egyptian remains. Without this expert conservation work, many old wall paintings and stone carvings would crumble away.

Tourism has damaged many ancient Egyptian remains. Moisture from visitors' breath and sweat has rotted fragile objects preserved in dry tombs for over 3000 years.

Archaeologists have used modern remote-control robot cameras to investigate narrow passageways deep inside pyramids and tombs.

Computers can be used to 'reconstruct' statues and buildings that have been damaged over the centuries. A computer can show what damaged stonework would have looked like when new.

The boy-pharaoh, Tutankhamun, died around 1343 BC. His tomb survived untouched. It was discovered in 1922, and shows us how rich Egyptian civilisation was.

Four shrines made of gold-covered wood, one inside the other

Antechamber, containing carved bed and guardian statues

Annexe

Gold coffin found in Tutankhamun's tomb. It is decorated with coloured glass and carnelian (a red semi-precious stone).

The last

pyramid was built around 2150 BC. Later pharaohs were buried in tombs in cliffs in the Valley of the Kings. These tombs were filled with treasures, but, in spite of hidden entrances and armed guards, most were robbed.

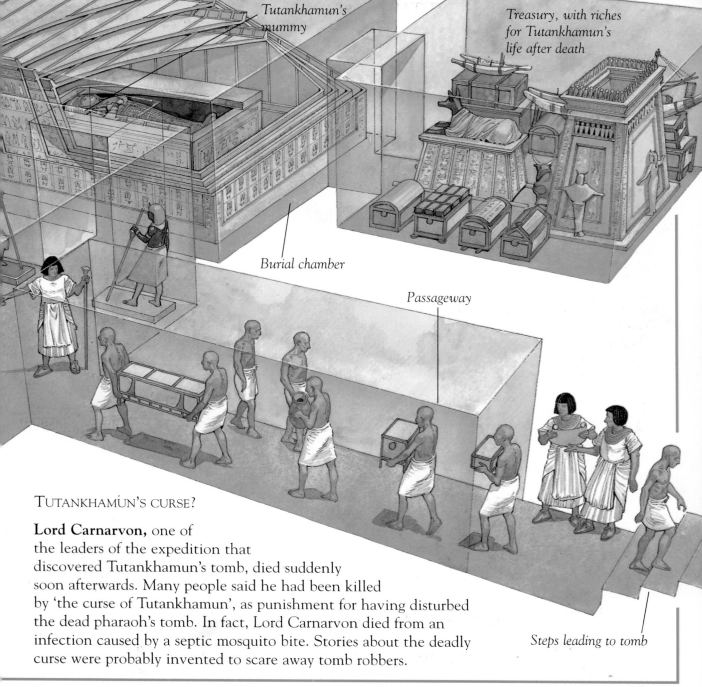

Tutankhamun's mummy

Treasury, with riches for Tutankhamun's life after death

Burial chamber

Passageway

TUTANKHAMUN'S CURSE?

Lord Carnarvon, one of
the leaders of the expedition that
discovered Tutankhamun's tomb, died suddenly
soon afterwards. Many people said he had been killed
by 'the curse of Tutankhamun', as punishment for having disturbed
the dead pharaoh's tomb. In fact, Lord Carnarvon died from an
infection caused by a septic mosquito bite. Stories about the deadly
curse were probably invented to scare away tomb robbers.

Steps leading to tomb

USEFUL WORDS

Archaeologist Someone who finds out about the past by studying its objects and buildings.

Amulet Small object believed to guard against evil. Often put inside mummies' coffins.

Canopic jars Containers to hold the lungs, liver, stomach and intestines of a body being mummified.

Embalming Preserving by soaking in resin or by wrapping in resin-soaked bandages.

Hieroglyphs Picture-writing, used by ancient Egyptian scribes. At first, each hieroglyph showed an object. Later, hieroglyphs came to stand for sounds, like letters in our alphabet.

Irrigation Bringing water to dry land.

Mummified Made into a mummy.

Natron A type of soda, found in the desert lands of Egypt. Used to dry dead bodies.

Papyrus A type of reed that grows beside the River Nile. It was used by Egyptians to make paper.

Pharaoh The ancient Egyptian word for king.

Scribes Government officials trained in reading, writing and keeping records.

Shrine Holy place where the statue of a god or goddess was kept.

Shroud Cloth used to wrap dead bodies.

Vizier The pharaoh's chief minister.

INDEX